How it began 2

By: Sirena Iorio

□ Chapter 1

It all began when Kassy's family was on their way. Looking out the window of her Chevy Malibu, her sun kissed strawberry blonde hair blowing in all directions like a lion's mane. The warm sun beat against her freckled tan skin. Her deep blue eyes wandering over all of Canada's great view. POP!! All of a sudden there was a loud banging sound. The car slowed to a stop with a piercing sound. There they sat silent. Kassy's big sister Jessa woke up and glared at Kassy. "Kassidy Leann Wentz! Now what did you do?" Jessa screamed. Kassy just sat silently. She knew her trip was ruined. There they all sat silent and motionless in Toronto Ontario Canada. Kassy tried to lift everybody's mood. "Come on its not that bad, I mean this place looks way better then Banff has ever looked plus we go there every year. This will be fun."

They got out of the car and grabbed their luggage. They found a nice place to stay and set their tents up. Kassy and her father went off on a hike. They walked around. They saw a little pond and walked over to it. There were ducks and ducklings, fish and flowers, bees and frogs. Kassy asked her father if she could get bread out of the picnic basket and give it to the ducks. Her dad agreed so she did exactly that. The ducks made their cute little sounds as they swam over.

Kassy sat down. She tossed little pieces of bread towards them and they gobbled it up. Kassy then got up. There she stood. She just watched the little ducks and their babies eat the bread. She turned to talk to her dad about the ducks and said, “Daddy, these ducks are soooo cute. Can I have one?” But her Dad wasn’t there! “Dad! Where are you? Yoo-hoo! Dad? Seriously! Where are you!”? Her Dad was gone!

Chapter 2

Kassy wandered on looking for her father and hit the big time town area of Toronto Ontario. She found a little piece of wood and sheltered herself. All of a sudden she heard a sniffing and panting sound! She freaked out! She looked out of the shack and saw her little dog. He must have followed her. "Dragon, come here boy" There came Dragon. He ran into the wood shack with Kassy and up on to her lap he jumped. He licked her nose and wagged his tail. Kassy was so happy to see her little boy. Kassy knew she had no way of finding her way back to their tents. She was so worried. She thought up a little tune while her dog twisted and turned in circles on her lap. She started humming it to her dog. While she was singing, a woman not much older then Kassy herself named Clarissa Bertone walked by. She heard a girl's voice that sounded not much younger than her own. Clarissa walked over to the shack and knocked on a piece of wood, which collapsed instantly. Kassy got all worried and answered, "Yes?" Clarissa pulled the wood… "What are you doing here?" "Oh, and that tune you are humming is well, pretty magnifical!" "Ha!" Kassy responded, "Why thank you. And I love that word ha magnifical it's like amazing." "Ha-ha why thank you, but I would really appreciate if you told me why you are here!" "ohh… right, well... it's a really long story." Kassy spoke embarrassed "well… what?" "Believe me I've got the time." Clarissa smiled and sat down. "Ok, well… here goes." "My family and I were on our way to Banff, then our car broke down. We were well pretty much stuck… blah blah blah blah blah. We found a place to stay were we set up our tents. My Dad and I went out to a pond and he walked off or someone like stole him and I walked here and found this gross piece of wood. I heard sniffing and apparently my dog followed me. And last but not least I'm here in this gross damp wood telling you my story. What if I never find my family?" She finished with a worried look on her face. Clarissa stood up and hugged her. “DON’T WORRY! We’ll find them. In the meantime, you can come and stay with me.” Kassy was so surprised to see that there were still nice people out here walking around town nonchalantly and she knew she was lucky because she herself had met the nicest one there is. And now she had made a new friend that she would stay with

Chapter 3

When Kassy got to Clarissa's home, Clarissa told her she had an extra room and to make herself at home. Kassy usually was an outgoing girl but at the moment she was really pretty shy. Kassy said to Clarissa, "Ok, I will!" "Oh, and thank you." "I can't thank you enough." Clarissa spoke in a soft tone. "Oh, you're welcome, and I forgot to ask" she added "is you at all hungry?" "I can make us up some warm soup." "Oh, ummmmm I'm okay thank you for asking though." Kassy lied. She knew she was very hungry but she just felt too bad especially because she was already at her house. She was really scared and really sad she missed her parents and even Jessa, but all at the same time she was so happy to be in that house. Kassy lie down and fell asleep.

Chapter 4

She woke up to the wonderful smell of homemade pancakes with blueberries. She walked out of her room. “Good morning Boo” said Clarissa. “Hi.” “How’d you know I go by Boo?” “Well I got a letter in the mail, and it said it was for me but really it was for you from your cousin.” “She seems very nice.” “Her name is Ginger.” “What?” “You boob!” “Give it to me!!!” “Whoa! This is a new side of you.” “We friends now?” “You’re a fun girl… pancakes?” she said childishly. Kassy got her phone out and texted ginger. She said “Hey Ginger.” “So glad we are now in contact.” “This is great and I’m soooo glad.” “Oh, yah btw this is Kassy!!! :).”

Kassy was so happy she didn't even eat her pancakes. Finally after a few long hours Ginger texted back and said "Hey boo!" "I <3 u!" "Omg! Can't wait till I move to Chicago! Well all this long distance texting is really starting to hurt my phone bill! Well we won't have to text a lot in Chicago when I move… so… ya! … luv ya!" Kassy called Ginger since Ginger had long distance calling. They talked for hours but when Kassy had to go she said "Bye love you sooo much" and Clarissa took her to the set she was working on. The producer/director asked Clarissa, "Who's the new girl?" "Oh, that's just a new friend of mine!" "Kay?" "So what part does she want?" "She is not here for a part, she is here with me." "She got lost so I'm with her and she is with me." "Ok." "That's strange, but she can't be here tell her to go outside." Clarissa went over to Kassy. She told her that she must go outside and that she was very sorry. Kassy said "Oh its cool see ya later alligator." Kassy walked outside. The big heavy door swung shut with a bang. Then out of nowhere the writer of "Fulfilling ~~Dreams~~ Death" ran into the room screaming "I can't believe it, this can't be real oh my gosh!" The producer ran over to her. "What's wrong?" "There's a girl out there!" "She's blonde, well strawberry blonde with blue eyes, she's tall, skinny and all natural and that's exactly what I wanted Milly to look like." "Is she in the movie?" Is that Milly?" "Umm" "No, we still have to hold the auditions for Milly." "Well if she can act she's got the part." "That's my choice, all out!" Clarissa just sat and smiled to herself.

Chapter 5

The writer of the movie, Marcy Graves runs over to Kassy and says, "Hi, I'm Marcy Graves." "I'm the writer of this movie and you, well you are exactly what I want Milly to be and I want you to try out and do you act or want to act because you are perfect… well for Milly of course." Kassy looked up from her phone confused since she had just been kicked out and said,

"Um, well, I'd love to thank you but I was just kicked out?" "Oh well ignore them. Come back and audition please! I'll give you $900."

“Whoa!, $900 really?” “Yah right hunny. $900,000 baby.” “Oh my gosh, I don’t know what to say.” “Well I’d I’d I’d love to try out,” she stuttered. Marcy gave Kassy a hand. Kassy stood up and dusted herself off. Back through the big heavy door they went. Marcy led Kassy into a dark room and told her she would be right back with the casting directors. Kassy looked around the room. She saw a long table that had many papers on it. She saw one mic. in front of her. The room was still and silent. The walls were painted very black. When Marcy came back three men and one woman followed behind her. They sat down at the panel. Marcy handed Kassy a script and went and sat down with the others.

Chapter 6

Kassy looked up at them then down at the script and back up at them. She started

"mother… papa…" She said in a worried tone as the script told her to "why, why, why'd you have to leave me the pain no dreams" the judges smiled they wanted to see her reaction for the next part Kassidy Leann Wentz dropped to her knees and screamed so high pitch that all the judges even Marcy plugged their ears they were all in awe. "Bravo!" "you rocked that" "dang girl you good u bada bada bad!" "great! You see that's the part was you get stabbed... no worries you live... sorta" Kassy was confused. "I get stabbed?" "Well yes." "Then you turn to a zombie." "Oh! Sounds, uh fun!" "Yes it really is! Your gonna be great!" "Does that mean I got the part?" "Yes, you did Milly" she said with a wink. Kassy ran out of the room and got her phone. She texted Ginger this: "Hwy." "Guess what?" "I got a part in the movie, Fulfilling D~~reams~~ Death." "I am Milly, the lead." Kassy had texted that so fast that the text was mixed with a bunch of random letters. Kassy ran over to Clarissa and told she had got the part. Clarissa was so happy that she hugged Kassy really tight and then told Kassy she knew she could do it. then Clarissa stepped back with a confused face. "Wait... you were only in there for about 5 minutes…" "Well ya!" "But she said I was perfect and she said the looks mostly and she said if I can act the least bit I got it but then she said I nailed it!" "Good job girly."

Chapter 7

The next day Kassy awoke it was the same routine. She woke up, had breakfast and went to the studio. She was learning her lines. It was difficult for Kassy because she had so little time and so many lines to learn. Kassy had a week left till they would start filming. She was hard at work. Two nights later Kassy got a call. She looked at her phone and it said Ginger. She ran to Clarissa and said "Come on!" "Let's go!" "We have to go." "Come on, we gotta get Ginger." Clarissa stood confused… "what are you talking about?" "… oh much gosh!" "Risa!" "Think about it why we came here to Chicago way before we even had to film here." "I told Ginger we were gonna be in Chicago soon… come on Risa!! Thinkkkk girl." "Ohhhhhhhhh!" "So we could see your cousin! Gotcha, isn't she going to stay in this hotel with us?" "Yes, she texted and called me and said she can't see us and asked were at the airport are we." "Oh well its fine we are only about two minutes away from there. Just call her and tell her we will be there any minute." So Kassy called Ginger and said exactly that. They stayed on the phone till Ginger was all the way in the car and off they drove. There they sat in silence until Clarissa said "well its 3:00 in the morning, I'm not quite sure what all we can do but I say we should call it an all-nighter. Then tomorrow we can go sightseeing and get to know cheecawgo ha!" Kassy and Ginger both thought that was a good no great idea. When they got to the hotel Ginger grabbed a Wii out of her many luggage bags and Kassy couldn't help but say "ohhhhhhhh! Girls let's just dance up this party!" Ginger said "oh you girls have got this all wrong! Three's not a party!" Ginger sent a text to five people and about fifteen minutes later Kassy dropped her Wii remote and ran to the door. Five girls came in they ran into the room and hugged Ginger., Kassy and even Clarissa. Ginger ran over to her bag and said "girls we all know what this means." She got the other remotes and they all danced even the ones without remotes. They had so much fun but then Kassy dropped her remote and ran into the bedroom she plopped onto the bed and started to cry. Ginger dropped her remote and ran after her. "Aww come on Boo, don't cry. Me and these girls are experienced that is the only reason we are beating you." "That's not it," said Kassy still crying "isn't there a little something your noticing Ginge? Jessa, my Mom and my Dad aren't here, I was lucky enough to be found by Risa on the side of the street in a shack thing in Canada!" "What are you talking about Boo?" "I was on a hike with Daddy in Ontario and I guess he wandered off when I was looking at the little ducks and I didn't know where to go I was looking and I guess I took a billion wrong turns and found myself in some huge part of Canada and I knew it wasn't Banff." Ginger stood up off the bed and hugged Kassy "It's ok Boo, why don't you call them?" "I don't have their numbers and my phone is at the tent. This is a phone from Clarissa, What if we never find them?" Ginger looked at Kassy with sympathy " Don't worry Hun, we'll find them."

Chapter 8

"Lets go back out with the girls Boo" Kassy stood up and hugged Ginger so tight. Ericka and Tiffany ran into the room and hugged them both then they pulled Kassy and Ginger into the dance memo. Jasmine and Alexis were dancing like crazy. They weren't even doing the right moves. Kassy looked over and Risa was making giant bowls full of popcorn. Ginger looked around and said "where did Natasha go?" Jasmine looked over her shoulder and said "she in da potty, she spilled Kool-Aid on herself, watta dork."Alexis added in "Did you know that a dork is a whales well ima stop there" and she danced on Natasha came out with her shirt that used to be white all red and splotchy they all started to laugh. Natasha ran over and hugged Kassy and said “Aww love you sooo much girly” and they danced on.

Chapter 9

Ginger ran and grabbed her phone when she got it she ran back out and said, “Kassidy, I have it! I have your Moms number in my phone we can call her!” Kassy grabbed Gingers phone and it started to ring. Her mom answered and said “hello. Who is this?” “mommy! It’s me Kassy I’m on Gingers phone!” “What baby? Where are you Jessa and I are worried sick!” “I’m with Ginger, Natasha, Clarissa, Tiffany, Jasmine and Ericka. I’m okay. I wanna come home. Oh and Mom, I’m starring in a movie!” “Oh that’s good! I want to come get you. Where are you?” “I’m in Chicago, you’re in, wait, are you home yet?" "What? Chicago? Jessa and I will come get you." "Wait, what about Dad?" "Baby, we don't know where he is you and your father never came back. We were hoping he was with you, but I.. i guess not." "Momma! what?" Kassy started to cry and Ginger took the phone and told Mrs. Wentz where they were and how to get there.

Chapter 10

Kassy woke up four days later with a knock on the door. She thought it might be room service. She opened it and there she saw them… Jessa and her Mother. Ginger walked out from the room and screamed they all ran and hugged each other. Kassy could not believe her eyes. She was so happy to see her Mom and even Jessa. Jessa wouldn't let go of her. She said to Kassy "Kassy, no matter what, you are my little baby girl and I will always love you." That was the nicest thing she had ever said to Kassy. Clarissa walked out and said "ok I really hate to break the love of you guys but umm Kassy has to film in thirty minutes." Kassy was so excited to show Jessa and her Mom the set, they went there and Kassy filmed her movie. That day was the wrap. Kassy had finished her movie, she had found her Mom and Sister and she was with all the ones she loved. Kassy was ready to go home with her $900,000 dollars she bought the tickets for her Mom Jessa and herself. She said goodbye to Ginger and Clarissa she left in tears. She was crying so hard people thought something was wrong with her. When the plane took off she looked out the window to try and see Ginger and Clarissa she wanted to wave to them one last time. But they were gone. She couldn't see them anywhere, her heart sunk and her eyes drooped.

Her mouth was in a frown and she was so sad she thought her life was over. She heard the airline lady walking down the aisle on the plane she wanted to buy some nuts. It seemed like she was in one spot for ever then Kassy felt a tap on her shoulder and thought finally I can get some food! She was starving she grabbed into her pocket for some money and took her ear buds out. She turned towards the lady and said one bag of nuts please with a smile. She paid her and rested back into her seat she looked to her left to ask her Mom if she wanted any but her mom wasn't there she was gone! Kassy couldn't believe this it couldn't happen again. She jumped up and hugged no one other then…

Clarissa, Ginger and even her father!

www.ingramcontent.com/pod-product-compliance
Ingram Content Group UK Ltd.
Pitfield, Milton Keynes, MK11 3LW, UK
UKHW041901190726
13854UKWH00003B/1017

9 781105 843761